T0196566

MARY ANN COLLINS

Order this book online at www.trafford.com
or email orders@trafford.com

Most Trafford titles are also available at major online book retailers.

Printed in the United States of America.

ISBN: 978-1-4669-4520-3 (sc)
ISBN: 978-1-4669-4519-7 (e)

Trafford rev. 09/24/2012

 www.trafford.com

North America & international
toll-free: 1 888 232 4444 (USA & Canada)
phone: 250 383 6864 ♦ fax: 812 355 4082

Contents

I acknowledge my husband, Gary R. Collins Sr.,
for helping me with my book.
To my daughter, Cashanita M. Walker,
for believing in me and giving me the encouragement
that I can do anything I put in mine to do.
To my sons, Eric D. Collins and
Gary R. Collins Jr., for supporting me.

I dedicate this book to my daughter
Cashanita M. Walker
and
in loving memory of my mother, Nellie L. Conley,
who passed away on May 29, 2012.

Chapter One

Learning to Adapt

O n a cold winter day, I was awakened by the whistling of the wind as it blew up against the apartment walls. It was Monday morning, a school day, and I really didn't want to get up.

I suddenly noticed my sister had her big feet on my stomach. She was trying to keep them warm.

"CeCe!" I yelled. "Get your big feet off my stomach!"

Unmoved, she was still lying there, like a lump on a log, so I pushed her feet off my stomach and rolled her over to the other side of the bed. I kept staring at her with a frown on my face because she knew that I didn't like it. She had done it before, and she'd do it again if she thought she could get away with it. My feet got cold at night, but I put socks on to keep them warm. I'd told her to put on socks too, but she wouldn't do it. I wished I had a bed of my own. Our bedroom was in the front of the apartment, and it was always cold. CeCe and I shared a full-size bed. I hated it with a passion.

Just then the alarm clock began to go off. I reached over, turned it off, and pulled myself out of the bed. Everyone in the house was asleep. I liked to get up first because they were all so slow.

I really slept hard last night. I could not see past the crust in my eyes. I stumbled into the bathroom to wash my face, and then I dried it. When I looked into the mirror, I had china eyes. I had been feeling really sad. I had been crying about Daddy again. I remembered dreaming about him last night. I rolled my eyes from the mirror, put toothpaste on my toothbrush, and began to brush my teeth. Then I poured mouthwash into a cup and began to gargle. I spit it into the sink and wiped my mouth with the back of my hand. Then once again, I began to think about him. I flopped down on the toilet seat and little tears came rolling down my face.

Then I began to say, "I was Daddy's little girl. We were so close. I don't even know what happened."

Daddy and I used to be the first ones up in the morning. He used to have a pot of coffee brewing when I opened my eyes. I could hear him singing and smell the coffee in my sleep. That's how I would wake up. He would be singing or humming a tune softly as he cooked breakfast, and I would join in. Sometimes he would bust out with a fancy move. He kept a smile on my face. While everyone slept, we would talk and laugh until we woke them up. It was my favorite time. He was so much fun. I really did miss him.

Suddenly I noticed the clock on the wall. I'd better get my brother and sister up, I thought. I was glad we had the alarm clock now. I learned, at an early age, not to depend on Momma. She used to oversleep all the time when Daddy was out of town on business trips. She would get up late for work and yell down the hall, "You kids, get up! Get up and hurry; you're going to be late for school!"

Actually, by then, we were already late. What made things worse, though, was that, when she rushed, she sometimes forgot things, like giving us lunch money. It was bad enough being late for school, but it was worse not having money for lunch. Our school made sure we'd have food to eat. I just hated asking. After a while, it just got really embarrassing. Daddy finally said we were old enough to have an alarm clock of our own. It made a difference in my life.

CeCe barely moved in the mornings. I liked to get her up last because, if I didn't, she'd just get in the way and make all of us late. Daddy said she was slow as molasses.

"Get up, CeCe! Come on; go wash your face," I said calmly. I pulled on her arm to get her going. She just curled up in a knot as usual. "Okay!" I said, frustrated. "Fine! I don't feel like it this morning, CeCe."

I made my way down to my brother's room. "Tim, get up," I said. "We're going to be late."

Tim rolled over, yawning, with his eyes closed. He said, "I'm up."

Finally everyone was up and getting ready for school. Momma was still asleep. We tried not to wake her.

Daddy was not with us anymore. Momma said he left her for another woman. It had been about two years now. I was in the ninth grade; CeCe was in the seventh; and Tim was in the sixth. Daddy said he would still take care of us and that he would always love us. I hadn't heard from him since.

Momma could not get past him leaving her. She kept drinking all the time. She finally lost her job and moved us into this low-income apartment. Over the past two years, she had often told us that Daddy did not want us anymore and that he did not care about us. After a while, I started to believe it.

Being in high school wasn't easy if you didn't have decent clothes. If I had a good friend, maybe I wouldn't feel so bad. There was Carol; she said she was my friend, but I knew she wasn't. She bragged all the time. She told me she looked better than I did. She asked me why I always wore the same clothes while she showed off her new clothes. That's why when I saw her coming, I turned around and went the other way.

After school, it was a challenge to come home. In the last six months, Momma hadn't been buying very much food. She was always drunk. I couldn't talk to her when she was like that, which was all the time. So I just stopped trying to talk to her. I did love my mother, but I didn't feel loved back. It was just Tim, CeCe, and me. I knew Tim and CeCe were very close to one another, closer than they were to me. They were always playing and having fun together. They had the same friends. I love my brother and sister more than they will ever know, I thought, shrugging my shoulders, and I choose to take care of them.

Most of my time at home was spent looking for food to eat in the kitchen. I knew how CeCe and Tim felt. What's the use? The refrigerator and cabinets are always empty. Many nights, we would go to bed hungry, and tonight was one of those nights. I peeped into Momma's room. Her liquor bottle was lying next to the bed, and she was out cold.

I went into the bedroom to do my homework and slammed the door behind me. "I'm just sick of this," I said to no one in particular. I started to think about how we hadn't gotten new clothes since Daddy left. I can't wait until I'm grown, I thought.

I put those thoughts out of my head, finished up with my homework and put something together to wear to school the next day. Then I took a bath and brushed my teeth. We all got ready for school at night so that, the next morning, we could hurry off to school. Daddy taught us that. We got free breakfast and lunch at school now, although I noticed that CeCe and Tim had extra money sometimes. I didn't know where they got it, and I had never asked. But I thought, good for them, and I tried not to feel sad for myself.

I was always the first one to go to bed at night. While lying down, I began to think about our situation. I didn't know why Momma would not go sign up for food stamps, or something, instead of lying around here day after day. I wouldn't be ashamed. I was tired of starving. Our mother needed help. She wasn't herself.

How could a mother starve her children? I thought. That's not caring for them. I would call the police, but we would end up in a foster home or separated from each other; that's what Momma said. I knew I wanted us to be a family. We all took care of Momma. When she was sober, she gave us money to go to the store to buy food. She was like a real mom then. Because of those days, I kept going.

Spring came and went, and so did Tim's birthday, which was on March 27. He turned twelve years old.

School would soon be out. Next week is my birthday, on May 10, and I will be fifteen years old, I thought as I walked down the school hallway to my class. I wanted to wear hot clothes this summer, styling clothes, but I knew it won't happen. Looking around, I saw some of the girls in school dressing nice and wearing fashionable styles. I wasn't jealous, but I was mad. With Daddy, we had nice clothes.

I couldn't think about anything else. I must have been daydreaming because the next thing I knew, Carol yelled, "Yolonda! I've been calling you. Are you okay?"

"Yes, I'm fine," I replied.

"Guess what? I like Tommy Moore, and I think he likes me too," she said, being sarcastic .

I really liked Tommy too. I was so surprised.

"Really? Good for you," I said . "Well, I'll see you. I'm going to stop right here and use the bathroom. Bye, Carol."

"Bye," she replied.

I rushed into the bathroom just to get away from her. I was really mad at her. I told her I liked Tommy. She did that on purpose. What's the use of having a friend when she stabs you in the back?

I looked at myself in the mirror. My clothes were old and simple; my socks had holes in them; and I needed a new pair of shoes. I thought, who would be interested in me anyway?

I was angry because I didn't think we had to live this way, and I let it get the best of me sometimes.

But it's all good, because I still have a home and a family, I thought.

Just then the bathroom door opened. I rushed out and hurried to my class.

One day, I got home first, and CeCe walked in wearing Momma's clothes.

"CeCe," I said, "you been in Momma's closet?"

"I've been wearing Momma's clothes. Where have you been? In la-la land?" she said. "If you think I'm going to keep wearing those old rags, then you keep thinking."

Looking at CeCe, I said, "You didn't ask her?"

"Londie, why are you so naïve?" said CeCe.

"What?" I said.

"What?" said CeCe. "You gonna wear the same thing over and over until it falls off you? How are you gonna keep going to school looking like that? Have you looked in Momma's closet lately? She has plenty of clothes in there, and she's not buying us anything."

Then CeCe walked past me to go into our bedroom, saying, "What she don't know won't hurt her."

I looked down at her feet; she was wearing Momma's shoes too. I felt so stupid. Momma wasn't home, so I opened her closet doors, and she had a closet full of brand-new clothes with the tags still on them! She's shopping for herself and punishing us, and for what? For being born? I thought.

It didn't take me long before I started wearing a blouse, a skirt, and mixing and matching stuff. I loved to model Momma's clothes in the mirror. I began to feel more comfortable at school. I could see people looking at me and giving me some compliments.

After school, I hurried home to take off Momma's clothes. I did know that if I got caught, I would be treated differently than CeCe. I wasn't Momma's favorite, but CeCe was. Maybe it was because Daddy and I were so close. Why do parents pick favorites and choose to love one child more than the other? I didn't believe Daddy did it, but Momma? She was another story. But I did love her.

The next day was my birthday; it was Saturday, and it was a beautiful day outside. I looked into Momma's room and saw that she was asleep. I closed her bedroom door softly. I was fifteen years old. I went into the living and sat on the couch to watch cartoons.

"Londie," said CeCe, "will you braid my hair?"

"Let's go outside," I said.

We sat on the steps outside of the apartment, and I French braided her hair.

"I can braid some hair!" I said when I finished.

"I like it," said CeCe.

After that, some of the kids around the apartment complex started paying me to braid their hair. I started buying food and other stuff. While out shopping, I decided to buy CeCe a necklace for her birthday. If it weren't for her, I wouldn't be making money at all, I thought.

Soon it was July 12, CeCe's birthday. She turned thirteen years old.

"Happy Birthday, CeCe," I said. I gave her the necklace.

"Thank you, Londie," she said. I gave her a hug. I helped her put it on. Tim went to the store to buy ice cream. I cooked dinner and baked and iced the cake. I popped popcorn, and we fell asleep watching TV in the living room.

As I slept, I began to dream about Tommy. He is so fine. I really do like him. But he doesn't even know I exist. I know I don't have a chance with him anyway. He has plenty of girls to choose from, including Carol. In my dream, I was told that I was a cute, brown-skinned girl, that I had a nice figure, that my hair looked good, that I always smelled good, and that my clothes were fresh and so clean. But then, I dreamt that my clothes were worn out, faded, and torn. Oh no! I started pulling and twisting on my clothes. When I woke up, I took a deep breath in and out. I had been dreaming. My blouse was twisted in a ball. I let my blouse go loose and got up.

CeCe and Tim were still asleep.

I went to bed.

As I lay there, I thought, since school is out, it doesn't matter what I wear. I'm enjoying it. Not that I have any place to go anyway. "This is summer vacation," I said, yawning, "and I'm loving it."

The next day, I overslept. CeCe and Tim were already gone. I went to the store to buy dinner. I had to clean up the popcorn mess. There was a ring around the bathtub, toothpaste in the sink, and the trash cans were full of trash. I am not the maid, I thought.

Later that evening, CeCe and Tim came home.

"CeCe, Tim," I said, "I know this is summer vacation. Do you have to be gone all day? There are chores that need to be done. I buy the food, cook, and do all the cleaning around here. I need you to help me."

"You're not our mother," said CeCe, "and you don't tell us what to do."

"I'm asking you to help me," I said.

"Londie, you don't have a life. All you do is sit around here all day in this house. You act like you're scared of people. You don't go out and try to meet anybody. You're boring and homely, and I'm ashamed to call you my sister. If I mess up, I'll clean up. I don't need you to tell me. Whatever you do around here, you choose to do. Just leave me alone."

"Yes, I choose too," I said.

"Nobody cares," said CeCe. "Why don't you just stop trying to be the momma? Because you're not."

"I'm not trying to be the momma," I said.

"Yell," says CeCe, being silly, and then she walked away. So did Tim.

Looking at Tim, I realized that he didn't have anything to say. CeCe normally did enough talking for the both of them. "You know, CeCe, whenever you want me to do something for you, I'm always there. But as soon as I ask you for something, you get an attitude."

"Well, if you just leave us alone, like I said, nobody cares what you do, Londie. Why don't you just mind your own business," said CeCe.

"CeCe—" I said.

Pointing her finger in my face, CeCe said, "Get yourself some business!"

Then she walked past me, into the bedroom, and slammed the door.

My feelings were so hurt. All I wanted to do was love and take care of her and Tim. Tim sat in the living room, watching TV.

"Tim," I said, "I just want to say I'm sorry. I love you and CeCe so much."

"Londie, it's fine to love us," said Tim, "but you can't control us. You're not too much older than we are."

"I know that, Tim," I said, "but CeCe seems to dislike me."

Tim got up and walked toward his bedroom. He turned to say, "Maybe she has a reason."

I sat in the living room, thinking and not really understanding what was going on with my brother and sister. I felt all alone. I expected to feel this way about Momma, but CeCe and Tim? They're all I have. I had no idea they felt this way about me.

Later, I turned the TV off and went to bed. CeCe was sound asleep, or pretended to be. As I lay there, I thought, I have no one, no one to love me at all

School would soon be starting. All summer, I had enjoyed having money in my pocket to spend. I love having money. I have got to find a job. That's the only way I'll survive, I thought. I was old enough to work. I decided I would start looking tomorrow.

Chapter Two

Consequences of Actions

Summer was gone, and school had started. I had no more money. I need bus fare to look for a job, I thought. Momma was always out of it in the morning. I went into her bedroom, looked inside her purse there beside the bed, and got money out for bus fare. To my surprise, there were two checks in her purse. I picked up the checks and eased them back into her purse. They were child-support checks.

Daddy said he would take care of us, but Momma was drinking it up. I wondered where she was getting money to buy her liquor and other things. She doesn't stay sober enough to do right by us. I find it hard to believe she gets out of bed to go buy this stuff, but she does. Look at these clothes in this closet. Her closet door was wide open. I thought she was so unfair, selfish, and mad at us because she was mad at our daddy. I really didn't care anymore. And I didn't feel bad about taking this money because it was ours too.

Daddy must still love us, I thought as I shut Momma's bedroom door, but he had another family. We would not fit in with his new family life. His new wife would not want us there, and I knew it would never work out.

The next morning, I left as if I were going to school. Instead, I went to the employment office, and they sent me to a company called the Diaper Service Company. If I were to get the job, I would be folding diapers, which would then be bagged and delivered to customers. I was hired on the spot. The hours were 4 p.m. to 8 p.m., Monday through Friday. I had a big smile on my face because I got a job.

"Yes!" I shouted as I walked out of the Diaper Service Company's building. I window-shopped until school was out. There were so many things I wanted to buy. I knew that CeCe and Tim would be happy. After all, this was for all of us. I couldn't wait to tell them the good news.

That evening, as we sat around watching TV, I said, "Tim, CeCe, guess what? I got a job. I'm so happy. I need you both to look after Momma and keep the house clean while I go to work."

There was a complete silence in the room. I looked at those two, and they said nothing. They continued to watch TV.

"Hey! What's wrong?" I said. "I'm going to buy school clothes for us."

"That's fine," said CeCe.

I looked at Tim, and he just shrugged his shoulders, never saying a word.

"You know, being the older one, I thought I could help us!" I yelled. "But you two, y'all act like you don't even care about anything. You know, I want some things; I want to eat! And you should too. I can't believe you two! I've been buying food and cooking."

I left the room mad. What's wrong with them? Sometimes those two really get on my nerves, I thought. Talking out loud, I began to say, "Being the older one, I am just trying to help. They are not happy for me or for themselves. I know I'm tired of not having food to eat. I don't care if we're wearing Momma's clothes; we have to eat. Besides, I'd rather have brand-new clothes of my own than wear Momma's. This job is for us."

They couldn't even look me in the face. Sometimes it gets hard, but how can I give up on my family, even though I know they have given up on me? I thought. I didn't tell them that Momma was getting the child-support checks from Daddy because, out of spite, I think they would have told Momma I said it. Trying to calm down, I thought, why do I get so upset? I know how they are.

I began to pace back and forth. "They probably would tell her, and the way Momma feels about me, I already know that I'm barely living here," I said. I laid my head down on the pillow because it began to hurt. It's true that my mother likes CeCe and Tim more than me. This place doesn't seem like my home anymore without Daddy. I closed my eyes, but I couldn't go to sleep. When CeCe came to bed, my eyes were just closed.

The next day, I took twenty dollars out of Momma's purse to get back and forth from work. If I had asked her for it, I do not know if she would have given it to me. She was not sharing the child-support money anyway. She was using it for herself. She probably won't miss it because she's drunk all the time, I thought. I know I am her child, and she is here with us. I think she would do better if she could. She just can't get over losing Daddy, I guess. She was hurting so bad that I could hear her cry at night in misery. She still loved our daddy, but Daddy had moved on. Sometimes I hated him for leaving us. It was very hard to look for him because he didn't even call.

I met several nice people at work. One of them was Karen Powell. She did not live far from me. She offered to pick me up and bring me home at night to keep me off the streets, and in return, I would help her with the gas on paydays. Just one week of working, and I have a ride to and from work. I am so happy. Yes! I thought. I did not have to take money out of Momma's purse anymore.

It was Friday, the last day of the week. Karen dropped me off, and I started running up the apartment stairs. I was so happy. I shouted, "Yes!" Everything is going to be all right, I thought. I got seven dollars an hour, and that sounded good to me. I started singing one of Daddy's old songs. "I love you for so many reasons. I love you for all seasons."

I put my key into the lock and opened the door.

There stood my mother, looking sober as she could be. Fear ran all over my body. CeCe and Tim were sitting at the kitchen table, sad and crying.

"Get your butt in here, and shut the door," she said calmly. "You have been taking money out of my purse." Before I could say a word, she slapped me across my face so hard that it brought tears to my eyes. I started holding my face because of the pain.

Then she started going off. "I knew I wasn't crazy; my money has been coming up missing for a long time," she said softly, pointing her finger at me. A long time? I thought to myself. I only took money out twice this week. I looked at CeCe and Tim and thought, I should have known; they've been taking money, too.

She then grabbed my face and turned it to look directly at her. "All my life," she said in a loud voice, "I've tried to do my best, but my best was never good enough—not for your daddy, not for my mother, and not for my father. It has always been my fault," she repeated. "I'm tired, and my own child is stealing from me. I'm tired! Everybody thinks I'm sick. Yes, I'm sick—sick of you, Londie. You're just like your daddy. You look like him, and you act like him. You want to work and take care of the kids? Fine! You take care of them, and you can raise them yourself, because I don't care anymore. But I will be damned if you're going to live here and take money from my purse. That's stealing, girl, from your own mother! It's my money. I earned it for my pain and suffering."

She let go of my face. Pointing her finger at me once again, she said softly and with daring, "You steal from me again, and I will kill you." I stood there and looked at Momma, her eyes filled with tears. We watched her as she stumbled back into her room. We all sighed with relief that she was gone. We could still hear her saying, "Do not steal from me," until she faded out.

Then I began to think that, even though I knew how Momma felt, she wasn't taking care of us anyway. But I didn't dare tell her that. This was our home with Momma. In my heart, I felt like she was really mad because we knew about the child-support checks. I didn't know why Momma felt like it all belonged to her. There were two checks for four hundred dollars in her purse—eight hundred dollars! Momma knew she was wrong. We had been starving, with no food to eat, and I had to go out and get a job, which I didn't really mind. But when I thought about it, Momma had been shopping for beautiful clothes, and she was probably eating well, and here, she had been letting us suffer. It's not like we did anything to her other than be born. Daddy left her, but we didn't; we were still here with her. I wondered how a mother could do this to her children. Maybe she had forgotten how to love anybody because Daddy left.

I knew CeCe and Tim were not innocent. I had only taken money out of Momma's purse two times. Maybe I took too much? I thought. I turned and looked at my brother and sister, and they looked at me. I wondered if they had put it all on me. They are always a step ahead of me, I thought. I'm tired and I'm so through with this. I'll take all the blame even though they know that I know they are guilty too. I went to my room and got dressed for bed. My head was hurting, and I just wanted to lie down. As I rested in bed, I started thinking about how Momma tried to make us feel like Daddy wasn't taking care of us and that she was doing everything by herself. Now I know the truth.

I was working every day. I bought us new clothes and groceries. It felt so good to be able to have money to spend. I had opened up a bank account. I gave Tim and CeCe money every day.

I buried myself in school and work. This is what I had to do. Sometimes I would fall asleep studying because I was so tired. On the weekends, I tried to do things with my brother and sister just to get out of the house. I found myself losing track of my surroundings.

I noticed Momma getting out more and not coming home at all. I couldn't remember when that began. I'd been trying to stay out of her way. I loved her, but I'd rather not tell her. I kind of felt good that she was getting out and meeting other people. I hoped she would get her life back together and get over Daddy.

Tim and CeCe, knew I loved them, and I felt it was my job to take care of them, but I sometimes wondered how they really felt about me. I believed they loved me. They took my money, but ever since that night with Momma, it had not been the same between us.

The months began to pass very fast. Thanksgiving Day arrived. I didn't know where Lorna, our mother, was. My job gave me a turkey, and I cooked it for the first time. CeCe made mashed potatoes and gravy, and I baked a cake. Everything was good. CeCe and I cleaned the kitchen, and we went to bed.

The next day, I went shopping for Christmas. It is very busy, I thought. I was told that the day after Thanksgiving is the best time to go shopping, but what a mess it was! People were everywhere. I actually had fun. I bought everything I needed for the presents. I brought out our little Christmas tree, decorated it, and put the presents under it. It was so pretty that it made me smile. CeCe and Tim looked very happy too.

Karen invited me to a Christmas program at her church. I remembered going to church when I was younger. I really liked it. This is something I can start doing with my brother and sister if I can get them to come, I thought. I did realize they were stubborn when they wanted to be.

Soon Christmas day came. I had to wake them up; I was so excited. Tim opened his present first. I got him this big ship to put together.

"You like it, Tim?" I said.

"It's cool," he said.

Then CeCe opened her present.

"I got you makeup because I know you use Momma's. How do you like it?" I asked.

"Thank you, Londie," said CeCe.

Suddenly I noticed I forgot about Momma. I was so busy shopping for my brother and sister that I forgot about her. Oh well, she isn't here anyway. I didn't expect her to be, I thought. I didn't know where my mother was. I didn't get anything for Christmas either, but I was okay with that because I'd go shopping for me after Christmas. I just enjoyed my brother and sister being happy. After Christmas, I went clothes shopping for myself and for them too. It was so much fun.

The months went by so fast. March 27 was Tim's birthday; he was thirteen years old. Tim and CeCe were nine months apart. They were almost like twins to me because they were so close. I could hardly see one without the other.

"Londie, I want to bake Tim a cake," said CeCe.

"Okay," I said, "I will go to the store and buy the cake mix, icing, and the ice cream."

"Get strawberry!" Tim shouted.

"Okay," I said. I put on my coat, hat, scarf, and gloves. When I opened the door, I said, "Ooh, It is bitterly cold out here." The wind blew and pushed me around all the way there and back. I bought dinner, and I cooked it, and we sat down and ate. Then we had ice cream and cake. Every now and then, I felt a shiver. It was still feeling cold to me. After washing dishes, I took a hot shower, and it steamed up the bathroom and that warmed me up. I put on my gown and some socks and went to bed.

Spring had finally come. Everything was blooming, and the birds were chirping. I was glad to see the cold weather go. I noticed that we would all need new coats for next winter. I guessed I'd start saving for that now. I also wanted to buy gloves and a knit hat too. I can put all that stuff in layaway, I thought. I sometimes wondered if CeCe and Tim appreciated all the things I did for them. I loved my brother and sister. I knew that I had taken on a lot of responsibilities, but what else could I do?

When I got to work on Monday, there was a mandatory meeting. The subject that interested me most was that all part-time employees could work full-time this summer. That meant more money and more s-h-o-p-p-i-n-g. Yes! I thought. Now we'd have money for new coats.

School would soon be out. It was my birthday. I got cake and ice cream at work. I took the cake home. Everything was going so well. I was so happy. I was sixteen and would be a junior next year. I decided I would buy some pretty clothes. Karen was going to be working full days too. She was going to be a sophomore in college.

Summer had finally come, and I started working days. I was so excited. Karen and I started eating lunch together. We had become good friends. The only time we would see each other was at work. I preferred it that way; I didn't want anyone to know that we were all alone.

One day, Karen asked me to have lunch with her and her boyfriend, James. When we got there, he had a friend with him named Arnold. James was very handsome. Karen talked about him all the time. He was tall and dark skinned. Arnold was also handsome. He was tall with a light-skinned complexion. They both wore jeans and T-shirts. They were both looking so fine. I caught myself staring at James at times, thinking to myself how good he looked. Then I saw Arnold, whose eyes were all over me. I felt so embarrassed. I could not enjoy my food because I was so uncomfortable.

We were at Bigger Burger Joint. They have great food. I wanted to pig out, but I couldn't, feeling the way I did. Look at him, I thought, staring me up and down. I'm sure this guy has a lot of experience with girls. I am not ugly, I know, and I'm dressing nice now. It seems that Arnold finds me attractive. Karen and I were both wearing jeans and tees too. We both had nice figures. I guessed we all looked very much like two couples, but not! I could not see Arnold being really interested in me since I was still in high school. He and James were both in college. I tried to get through the meal as best I could by paying attention to the conversation. After a while, he stopped looking like such a bad person. I'll give him a chance, I thought. But I still wasn't sure because he was so persistent.

We got to know each other, and I agreed to see him again. But I felt kind of pressured. He asked me for my phone number, and I gave it to him, and he gave me his. They walked us out to Karen's car, and on our way back to work, Karen asked, "So what do you think about Arnold?"

"He's okay," I said.

We didn't say much more as we hurried back to work. I believed she sensed I was mad at her. I thought to myself that she had been wrong not to tell me she was setting me up with a man. Even when she took me home from work, I really didn't have much to say to her.

"You're quiet," she said.

"I'm tired," I replied. "Bye."

Then I closed her car door and hurried across the courtyard. I heard her say, "Bye," softly, but I didn't care to look at her. I was mad.

As soon as I got in the door, the phone was ringing.

"Hello," I said. "May I speak to Yolonda?"

"This is Yolonda," I said.

"This is Arnold. I'm glad you gave me your number," he said.

The conversation went on for about an hour. It was nice to talk to a boy, I thought as I hung up the phone. CeCe and Tim were very quiet, watching TV. I was tired, so they were going to have to fend for themselves and find their own food tonight. I went to bed.

He called me every day. He made me laugh, especially when he was silly. He wanted to come over to see me, but I wasn't sure. He might find out our secret. I couldn't let that get out.

He became pushy and persistent. He started making me mad. I felt like he was trying to tell me what to do, so I kept telling him no all the time, although I thought of him as a friend. When he called me his girlfriend, I corrected him and told him I was not.

After a couple weeks, I decided to let him come over. I wasn't sure, but I said okay anyway. I was trying to get to know him. I was tired of him asking to see me and me not giving him a chance. He knocked on the door, and I let him in. I offered him a seat, but he did not sit. He started looking around and being nosy.

"Arnold, have a seat," I said.

Ignoring me, he asked, "Where is your mother?"

"Arnold, you came to see me. That's none of your business," I said.

He suddenly saw a picture on the wall.

"Is this your mother?" he asked.

I said, "Yes, that is my mother."

"I've seen her somewhere," he said.

Oh, this will not work, I thought. I suddenly realized I had made a mistake letting him come over.

"I'm sure I have," he said.

I started trying to get rid of him, so I pushed him along. "Arnold, I've got things to do, so I'd better get started. I'll call you tomorrow," I said, lying and pushing him toward the door.

He grabbed both of my hands and said, "Yolonda, you're lying. You have never called me. I'm not ready to go." He pulled me close to him and kissed me so passionately.

I felt so scared about how to get him to leave.

"I just got here, Yolonda," he said, but I continued to push him out the door. "Fine," he said, throwing his hands up in the air. "I'm leaving."

We said our good-byes. I thought to myself, and good riddance. Arnold was more than I could handle. I didn't know if it would work out after all. I was glad I got him out of here. Next time, I might not be so lucky. I had to be careful with him because I didn't want him to take advantage of me. I really didn't want to see him anymore. This guy has surely been around, I thought. He had experience with girls; I could tell. I decided I had better leave him alone. I had to think about CeCe and Tim and set a good example for them.

I had been working full-time, saving money for our winter coats and school clothes. It was going to be a good year for us with new stuff. I was so happy.

Before I knew it, it was July 12, CeCe's birthday. She was fourteen. I baked a cake for her. Ice cream was in the freezer. Actually, I haven't seen her or Tim this morning, I thought, looking out the window. They have really grown up. One thing I was happy about was that someone was paying the electric bills and the rent around here, although I was buying the groceries.

I had to be at work at eight o'clock, so I hurried off. That evening, I was so tired that I barely said a word to CeCe and Tim. I went straight to bed.

Chapter Three

An Eye-Opening Experience

chool was about to start. It was Friday evening. I'd been avoiding Arnold all summer. He called, but I never invited him over. I'd known him a few months now, but I still didn't trust him at all. He called me "one of his ladies." I actually thought he was crazy. I only talked to him because he called continually. I'd asked him to leave me alone, but he acted like he didn't hear me. I knew he had an agenda, and I was scared of him.

I thought about Momma. I needed her more than ever now. I felt like she had a new home and had left us too. She knew that she was all we had. I guessed she really meant for me to raise the kids. I guessed that was exactly what I was doing. I flopped on the sofa; I was so angry. Then the teardrops started to fall. I was tired. She had really made me mad. Soon the little tears became a waterfall. I was crying so hard. I ran to the bathroom to get tissue to blow my nose.

Suddenly there was a knock on the door. I tried to wipe all the tears from my eyes before answering it. I was on my way to the door when there was another thump, thump on the door. "Okay," I yelled. It must be CeCe or Tim, I thought. "Hold on, where is your key?" I yelled. I swung the door open, and there he stood: Arnold. I was so nervous, I felt the urge to pee.

"Arnold," I said. "What are you doing here?"

His strong cologne hit me all up in my nose as he approached me. "I've been thinking about you a lot, Yolonda," he said.

"Arnold, I've been trying to tell you it's over," I said in a hateful way. "And you didn't listen. We were only friends. We never did go together. And didn't you put enough cologne on?" I said, pinching my nose.

He pushed his way in, uninvited, and closed the door behind him.

"Hold, hold on," I said, holding out my hand and pressing it against his chest. "Arnold, I didn't invite you in. You have to leave."

"Why?" he said.

"Because it won't work, you and me," I said, "and mainly because you don't listen. I've got a lot on my mind right now, and this is not the best time."

"So when will be?" he said.

Looking at him in confusion, I yelled, "Arnold, will you please leave!" He wouldn't take no for an answer; I could see that.

Ignoring me, he said, "Yolonda, you've been crying." He reached out his hand and touched my face, and I hit his hand. Then he tried to kiss me. I pushed back from him and held my hands out toward him.

I was angry, and there was also anger in my voice as I told him again to please leave.

"Are you home alone?" he asked. "Where are your brother and sister? Will they be coming home soon? What about your mother? Have you seen her lately? I know that you are home alone, Londie. I've been watching you," he said aggressively. About this time, he was all in my face.

The look on my face showed how I hated him. "I hate you! Get out! Get out of here!"

I screamed. I tried to walk past him to open the door, but he lifted me up. I kicked and screamed for him to put me down, but he carried me to my bedroom. When he put me down, I smacked him as hard as I could on his face. I knew I was making him angry because it showed all over his face, but I didn't care.

Suddenly he grabbed me and threw me down on my bed. I fought him with everything I had. I tried to bite and scratch him and repeatedly told him no. But he pinned me down, and he raped me. It burned like fire. I began screaming out of control because he hurt me.

Finally it ended. My head ached like he had smacked me in the head, but I didn't remember if he had done that. I felt beat up. My skin was burning from scratches. My feelings were hurt. I was angry and in pain. As I lay there, weak and in a daze, he lay on top of me.

Then I heard a voice say, "Londie, I'm pregnant." It was CeCe, and she was crying. I managed to push him off of me. I got up limping, and quickly grabbed a robe and put it on, holding onto my stomach. I reached out to her and gave her a hug. Then he got up, dressed, and left.

I could hear the front door shut. I thought to myself, finally.

"CeCe, we will get through this together," I said. "I am your sister, I love you, and I will always be there for you."

I walked her to Momma's room, put her to bed, and took a long, hot bath. I was feeling bad myself. I was burning inside and out. I thought to myself, could it be true, CeCe pregnant? She's just a kid. I didn't even know she was having sex. I wonder who the father is. I wonder if he will help her. Then reality hit me that I was just raped and could be pregnant too. But whom could we tell? We're all alone, and we can't tell anyone because we will be taken from our home.

I got out of the tub and dried off, looking down at my stomach. I will kill him, I thought, if I am. I looked into the mirror, and yes, I had scratches and bruises on my face, but I wanted to be strong for CeCe. I got dressed for bed and took two pain pills and curled up into a ball until I fell asleep.

The next morning was Saturday. I lay in bed, feeling bad. My body still ached with pain. I got up to go to the bathroom and there I saw CeCe, throwing up in the toilet. After she had finished, I gave her a warm washcloth to wash her mouth. She gargled with mouthwash and went back to bed. I took two pain pills, got dressed, and gathered some strength to walk to the grocery store to buy a home pregnancy test. The test did confirm the pregnancy. I knew we couldn't afford a doctor.

"It's going to be all right," I told her. I gave her a hug, and she hugged me too. Our eyes were watery. I knew CeCe depended on me. I didn't know what to do, but I knew I would be by her side through this.

This was the last weekend before school started. We had all planned to go school shopping, but instead, Tim and I went. We left CeCe at home in case she needed to go to the bathroom to throw up. She wasn't showing yet, but I still bought her clothes in a bigger size. She did not know how far along she was. We were going on for now, as if nothing was wrong.

We laid around all day Sunday; we didn't know what else to do. We went to school on the first day, and after school, I went to work from 4 to 8 p.m. again. I didn't see Karen, nor did I look for her. I had to be strong.

It was so sad that we were all alone. Momma just disappeared, and Daddy was with his new family. He did not ever call. Grandma Penn, Daddy's mother, was in a nursing home. She really did love us. I missed her so much. She had Alzheimer's disease, and did not remember us anymore. I did not know how to contact my mother's parents. They lived out of town. Momma never talked about them. I guessed she did not want us to know them. I remembered Momma and Daddy fighting all the time about them.

Momma hit Daddy with brass knuckles in his jaw once.

Daddy said that was it. He left Momma that night and never came back. Things got really bad for us after that. I wondered if Momma regretted hitting him because he finally left her. He couldn't take it; now they were both gone.

A half hour had passed. I had spent all that time daydreaming. It was getting late, but I wanted to go to the store to buy oil to fry chicken that I had set out to thaw.

"I'm going to the store," I told Tim and CeCe. I walked slowly down the apartment steps into the courtyard. As I approached the store, I could see my mother. She was bending over into a car. She was talking to the man in the car. She was all dressed up from head to toe. Momma had enough clothes in her closet, but the outfit she wore was a new one.

The car pulled off, and another one pulled up to her. Momma bent down to talk to the man. I had to see her and talk to her, so I began to walk slowly over to her. It looked like my mother was prostituting. I looked around, and there were a lot of people. They were staring at her and talking. When the last car took off, I bravely walked closer to her.

"Momma, Momma," I called. My heart was beating so fast. The slender person wearing leather shorts and boots turned and looked at me. She had beautiful long hair and long nails. She was just gorgeous.

"Londie," she said.

"Yes, Momma" I answered. "Will you come home with me? It's very important." I was talking so fast. Standing there for a second, my mother just looked at me, with tears running down my face. "Mother," I said, "Come home; we miss you." I walked over to her and gave her a hug, and she hugged me back.

I grabbed her by the hand, and my mother and I walked back to the apartment.

It felt so good to have Momma home again. Momma and I talked for hours, and we didn't mention her being gone at all. I didn't mention our problems here at home. I was waiting for the right time, but I didn't know when that was. I was talking to my mom. It felt like a dream.

We had peanut butter and jelly for dinner, and it was good. I noticed CeCe shying off and Tim not saying much. I didn't know what their problem was. I was glad to have Momma home. CeCe slept with me that night, and Momma had her old bed back.

The next morning, Momma was nowhere to be found. All the stuff I had in my purse was dumped on the kitchen table. I know she didn't take my money, I thought. But I was wrong. Is this payback? I was glad I had a little money in the bank. At that moment, I knew what it felt like to have someone take money from me. Was Momma teaching me a lesson? I thought. I could not get mad, but in my heart, I was sad.

I got CeCe and Tim up. "Momma is gone again," I said. "I am missing money. Everything I had in my purse is dumped out onto the table. Do you know why? Did you see anything?" I asked.

CeCe just looked at me and turned around and started getting ready for school. Tim just looked out the window in a daze. Our mother had left again, and no one said a mumbling word. I stood in silence too, thinking to myself, what else can happen?

We all went to school; no one said a word. It was very hard for me. I wished I could go back to the day before I saw my mother picking up men. I decided never to tell Tim and CeCe. They did not need to know that about our mother, and it was too embarrassing to talk about anyway. Suddenly I remembered something Arnold had said that he had seen my mother somewhere. Could he have seen Momma on the streets? I sat down at my desk and placed my hand on my head. Arnold had seen my mother on the streets, prostituting, I thought.

I was staring out the window, and suddenly I felt ill. I was tired of being a mom. I was tired of working. I was tired of being the only one who seemed to care. I went home early from school. I went to bed and had a terrible nightmare. I dreamt that I was fighting to protect myself. It was so overwhelming that I woke up in a deep sweat. I got up and noticed that school was out. Looking out the kitchen window, into the courtyard, I could see Tim talking to those bad boys who are in trouble all the time. I thought to myself, What's going on? Things are really getting out of hand. We need our mother here. I'm going to take off work today and hang around to see what's going on. I wasn't feeling good anyway.

Later we ate ice cream and cake. CeCe helped me clean up the kitchen, and then she went to her bedroom. Tim was watching TV. I called in sick, but I pretended to go to work. I hid outside and waited for hours in front of the apartment. It was about 6:30 p.m.; nothing was going on. I began to feel tired and sleepy, so I went around the back and went up the back stairs, feeling so stupid for thinking that something was going on. I turned my key and opened the door. The apartment was quiet. I peeped into CeCe's room and then into Tim's room. They both were gone.

Suddenly there was a knock on the door. I looked at the clock; it was 6:45 p.m. "Who is it," I said. There was no answer. I slowly opened the door.

Before I could say another word, a man said, "You got the goods." The guy was handing me money.

"What goods?" I said. I looked at him so confused, and he took off. I quickly closed the door. What just happened? I thought. I was really scared.

It was seven o'clock when I noticed that I was walking around in circles and talking to myself. I'm too young for this, I thought. Where is CeCe? Where is Tim? Then I heard someone putting the key into the front door. I ran to my bedroom with the door cracked to see who it was. CeCe walked in dressed in Momma's clothes. She had on this orange skirt, which was as high as her butt. She knows she can't wear that skirt. Her butt is too big. She had on a shear purple blouse with Momma's black boots that went up her legs. Her face was painted with a little glow to it. She reached in her bra and pulled out some money and began to count it as she walked passed my bedroom. My sister has been out prostituting! That's probably how she got pregnant.

Just then I heard the front door open again. I could hear Tim talking to someone.

"Hold my gun over here tonight, man," someone said.

"I got it," said Tim. It sounds like Brad, one of the boys who is always in trouble, I thought.

"You got the goods too," he said.

"Right here," said Tim.

"All right man, I'll see you tomorrow," he said.

"Right," said Tim. Then I heard Trouble say, "Hey, tell CeCe she looked lovely tonight." Then I heard the front door shut.

I put my hands over my face. I was a failure. I admitted that I was tired. I was so glad I stayed home instead of going to work. CeCe and Tim had involved themselves in something dangerous. I could not help them anymore. I was not their mother.

Chapter Four

Enough

The next morning, we all got up, like any other day. I hadn't slept during the night. I looked at my two siblings; they looked so innocent. I gave them lunch money, like I normally did, and they both took it, even though and I now knew they had money.

Ceaira, our CeCe, was fourteen, and Timothy was thirteen, and both of them were big-time hustlers. I hoped they didn't catch me staring at them. This was all so shocking to me. But did I dare let them know that I knew? Who am I? I thought; I'm just their big sister and that's all. This is way out of my hands. I have to figure out what to do about it. They are in pretty deep trouble from what I could see last night. I have to do something.

They went off to school and left me at home. I pretend to feel sick. After they were gone, I went into Momma's room and started going through all her personal things. I was looking for a number to locate Daddy. He was our only hope. What a fool I was to think that I could take care of my brother and sister by myself. One thing I could say about us was that we knew how to survive. I caught myself daydreaming again about how this could have happened. I hoped that I was not too late. There wasn't anything with Daddy's name on it. I called directory assistance, but I did not know the address. I got the telephone book and started looking for George and Sheila Penn's address, but I found none. I called a couple numbers, but no one answered.

I'd been trashing the apartment all morning. Then I went back into Momma's room. Where had I not looked? I turned over the mattress. I pulled the dresser drawers out. I checked the top shelf in the closet. I knew Momma had to have a number to reach Daddy somewhere. This was harder than I had thought. I turned the bottom of the dresser drawer over and there, taped to the bottom of the drawer, were pictures of CeCe nude. Yuck, I could not believe what I was seeing. I slowly pulled the taped pictures off the drawer. Then I let them fall from my hands, and I kicked them under the dresser.

I felt so confused. I was so tired of looking. As I looked across the room, I saw something hanging on the wall behind the closet door. I walked over to it, and I saw life insurance policies for Ceaira Jalisa, Timothy Jaudon, and Yolonda Judith Penn. In the envelope, I found a number for George F. Penn at 3525 La Mead Street. I dialed the number, but no one answered. A voice message said, "Hi, you've reached the Penns. Sorry we're not home. Please leave a message, and we'll be sure to call you back." I hung up the phone. I called the bus company to find out how to get there. It was ten minutes after one o'clock. I hurried to catch the 1:25 bus. I was on the bus; my heart started to pound fast. The houses began to look so beautiful along the way. Suddenly the bus driver started to turn off the route. It was 1:45 when I looked at my watch.

"Excuse me," I said. "Is this as far as you go?"

"Yes, miss," he said. "This is the end of my route."

"I need to get to 3525 La Mead Street. Can you help me?" I asked.

"That is a couple miles up the street. When you see Talton Street, La Mead Street should be very close," said the bus driver.

I got off the bus. I was so mad. But I didn't want the bus driver to see me cry. I wasn't going to cry this time. I squirted two big tears out of my eyes and wiped my face on my blouse. I'd come too far to give up now.

It was 2:15. Before I knew it, I was at Talton Street. I kept on walking about five more blocks, and I saw La Mead Street. Finally, I arrived at 2:25. I began to feel scared. The houses looked very nice here at West Ridge Manor. My heart began to pound really hard as I reached the address. I stepped up to the door and knocked. Then I rang the doorbell. I knew no one was at home, so I sat down with my head in my lap.

As I sat there, in deep thought about everything that had gone on, a white lady approached me. "Hello," she said. "Can I help you?"

"Yes," I said. "I am looking for my daddy, George Penn."

"Well, he's not here right now; he is at work," she said nicely. "Are you Yolonda?" she asked.

"Yes, ma'am," I said.

The lady reached out and shook my hand and said, "My name is Alma. I'm glad to meet you."

"Glad to meet you too," I said.

"Your daddy talks about you all the time. Come on over to my house. I will call him," she said.

I walked with the woman to her house, and she called my dad and told me he was on his way.

She offered me food and water, but I said, "No thank you," even though I was hungry and thirsty. I was so nervous. Within twenty minutes, the doorbell rang. In walked my daddy, and he reached out his hands, and I ran to him with tears flowing and gave him the biggest hug. My daddy wiped my tears from my eyes, and he said, "Londie, you're home." He thanked the lady next door, and I thanked her too. Daddy and I went over to his house. His home was as lovely inside as outside.

We talked, and I told him everything. I asked him why he did not come and get us sooner. He said that Lorna, our mother, told him to stay out of her life and that she had a new man and not to bother seeing us kids.

"Daddy, you get home visits, don't you?" I said. "We are your kids too. If you had just come by, you would have seen for yourself."

"I know, honey," said Daddy. "I guess I didn't want to see Lorna and the hurt in her eyes. It burned deep in her, the sorrow we both shared, and I know that's not a good excuse, but it's the only one I have."

"Daddy, what are you talking about?" I said.

"We had this big fight the last time I was with her. She hit me with some brass knuckles, and I hit her back. I know I should not have done that. I really felt bad about it. She then filed a restraining order against me. I was ordered by the court to pay child support. I didn't want to get into any more trouble, so I just stayed away. Lorna was drinking and acting a fool, and we just weren't getting along," he said.

"Daddy, if you knew she was doing that, then why did you leave us with her?" I said.

"I hit Lorna, the woman I love," he said. "I knew what she was going through, and my presence there made it worse. I did not believe otherwise. I didn't want to take you kids from her too."

I knew Daddy was not lying because I had seen the child-support checks. "Daddy," I asked, "why didn't you call?"

"I do, honey," he said, "I talk to CeCe and Tim all the time. I heard that you were working, which I thought was very good."

"Really?" I said. How could they not tell me about Daddy calling? I thought. "Daddy, did they ever tell you that Momma had left us," I asked.

"No, they did not," he said. "When I would ask to speak to her, she was never there, but I didn't think that she was gone."

"Londie," he said, "I have made a big mistake by not checking on you. I see that now. I hope you will forgive me. I never thought that CeCe and Tim were not telling me everything. I just took it for granted that everything was all right."

"Me too, Daddy," I said. "I guess I am just like you." I gave him another big hug. At that moment, I felt some of the pressure being lifted off my shoulders.

Daddy and I went to the apartment. On the way, he said that he had already talked to his new wife, Sheila, and she did want us to come and stay.

School was out. We arrived before CeCe and Tim. We waited patiently. When they walked through the door, CeCe appeared first. She was already showing a little bit, and then Tim came in after her. They had really grown up. They looked at Daddy in amazement.

Daddy said, "I've come to take you all home."

Looking surprised, CeCe said, "Why now?"

"Because it's overdue," said Daddy.

Looking him up and down, CeCe said, "I can't." Then she moved her head from side to side and put her hands on her hips.

"Yes, you can," said Daddy.

"You never cared before," she said.

"CeCe, I've talked to you all the time; you never told me anything negative. How was I supposed to know?" said Daddy.

At about this time, I sat down and put my face in my hands and my elbow on my lap to hold me up. I took a deep breath because I was so tired. As I looked on, CeCe pointed her finger at Daddy and yelled, "You're supposed to be the daddy!"

"I am the daddy, your father, and I'm taking you home with me because I care. I know everything now. I can't leave you here," said Daddy.

She walked over to him and said, "I'm fat and ugly."

Daddy said, "You're my little girl, CeCe, and you're pretty to me. I love you so."

She gave him a hug with tears in her eyes. She said, "I love you too, Daddy."

I looked over at Tim. He was so quiet.

"Tim," Daddy said, "Son, how about it?"

"I hate you," he said. "A dad doesn't leave his kids."

"I was always a phone call away," said Dad. "And you know that. I gave you my phone number to call me anytime."

"It's too late. You can't come in here and make changes," said Tim.

"Tim," Daddy said, "I only have a little time with you, Son, before you are a grown man."

"I'm a man now," said Tim, with his face puffy.

"You've grown a lot, Tim, I can't deny that," said Dad. "But I'm here now, and I'm taking over the responsibilities. I'm human, and I have made mistakes. But, Tim, as long as you live, you will make mistakes, too. If you don't learn from them, you may fail in life. Don't you see? I've been given a second chance. And, Tim, if you are ever given that opportunity, you need to correct your mistakes just like I'm trying to do now. When I said I did not know, that's my fault for not finding out; I'm sorry, Son. But now that I know, I want my family back. Tim, I will always be your dad and you my son, and you can't change that. I'm not just here talking; I'm here to take you home. So please, Son." He held out his hand to Tim.

I could see Tim's lips balling up, and his fist became a knot. He looked angry, like he wanted to fight. Daddy still reached out his hand. CeCe and I looked on. Then Tim reached out and took Daddy's hand, and they both embraced. What a relief, I thought. As I looked around, everybody's eyes were filled with tears.

We started packing that day to move into Daddy and Sheila's house. It was uncomfortable at first for us, but Sheila was very nice, and she made us feel at home. The house was clean and homey. This was what I had always wanted, a loving, caring family with Daddy again. I thought, it's unbelievable. We put everything in the basement for the moment. It was going to take some time to get our stuff organized. We were all tired and ready to go to bed.

We knew it would take some time to get used to all of this, but I was willing to try and so were my brother and sister. CeCe and I were sharing a room again, but that was okay. We both had our own separate beds, Yes! I thought, that makes all the difference. Tim had his own room, and our baby brother, Aaron, who was thirteen months old, slept in the room with Dad and Sheila. They had their work cut out for them, but I really admired Sheila for it.

Just then, after everything calmed down, I remembered Daddy saying he had talked to CeCe and Tim all the time. Those two knew all along how to get help, and they never even tried. All the suffering we went through, and Daddy was only a phone call away. I knew they had secrets and didn't include me. It was like they hated me or something. They were willing to be destroyed instead of reaching out for help. They truly wear me out. I guess I have to finally admit that I don't understand them. I felt used. I took a deep breath and made a sign of relief. Then I thought, they are not my problem anymore. They had Dad and Sheila.

Chapter Five

The Guilty

*T*he first night, I lay down in my bed, feeling relaxed. My eyes were very heavy, and I closed them to go to sleep.

"Londie," said CeCe, "are you asleep?"

"No," I said.

"Tim and I, we kept a lot of secrets from you," she said. "We felt like you were always trying to boss us around just because you are the oldest. So we decided to do whatever we wanted, no matter what you said. We called you 'Miss Goody Two Shoes' and 'Miss Know It All.' We wanted you to get in trouble with Momma. We didn't want you to talk to Daddy for one reason, which was that you are Daddy's girl. We knew what Momma was doing. She was prostituting and on drugs, and I wanted to be just like her. I wanted to be Momma's little girl. You see, Momma, she understood me. She knew just what I needed. And I didn't want it from you, Londie. All you ever thought about was work and bossing us around. You were not our Momma. You were just the oldest one, trying to throw your weight around, and Tim and I didn't like it."

I sat up in the bed and turned and looked at CeCe. Then I heard the sniffles; CeCe was crying.

"CeCe, are you telling me Momma knew what you and Tim were doing?" I asked.

"No, we hid it from her," said CeCe. "She told me and Tim not to do it."

I got up and sat on the side of the bed next to CeCe and said, "It's going to be all right now. Everything I did was for you, Tim, and me. I know you and Tim are close, and I accept that. I was only trying to hold our family together because nobody else was. I wasn't trying to be bossy or the momma. It was because I love you and Tim." I wrapped my arms around her and gave her a hug.

"I know that now, Londie," said CeCe. "Londie, you won't love me after I tell you this, but I turned Momma against you. I lied about you. I wanted Momma to love me more. I wanted you to hurt and to get into trouble. I envied you. Tim and I hated you. I was out there on the streets, and I thought it was okay because Momma was doing it. It put money in my pockets. I thought it was the only way to survive."

"It's okay, CeCe," I said. "I know. Go to bed." I kissed her on the cheek. "Go to sleep, everything is all right now." I walked over to my bed and lay back down to go to sleep.

"Londie," said CeCe, "I set you up."

My eyes opened wide again. I sat up in the bed. "Set me up? What do mean, CeCe?" I said.

"You know the day you got raped?" she said. "I didn't know he was going to do that."

"What are you saying?" I said, climbing out of bed. I began to walk toward her. "What did you say?"

"He said he just wanted to talk to you," said CeCe.

I found my hands reaching for her, and she began to kick at me. I caught her by her gown and grabbed her up before I realized what I was doing. I saw her big stomach, and I let her go.

"Don't hit me, Londie," she said. She proceeded to say, "I'm sorry. When I saw you all beat up—I'm sorry, Londie."

Tears began to roll down my face, and she began to cry too.

"No matter how I felt about you, I didn't want you to get raped and beat up," she said, getting out of bed.

"You know I was there for you, CeCe, when you said you were pregnant. I got right up to help you after I was raped and in pain. I took care of you. You gave it away for money. He beat me up, and I was all alone. I could not fight him by myself, and you could have helped me. You're sorry? You're sorry!" I screamed.

I balled my fist up, and CeCe ran to her bed, grabbed a pillow, and held it tightly around her stomach.

"I'm not gonna hit you, CeCe, but I promise you, if you weren't pregnant, I would," I said. "I have never felt so bad in my life. Betrayed by my own sister. I am so hurt." I turned and walked away.

Holding my head, I could feel a terrible headache coming on, so I lay my head down on my pillow. She continued to talk.

"Londie," said CeCe, "I promise I will be a better sister. Tim and I, we do love you."

"Shut up CeCe, Tim is not here confessing, you are," I said angrily. "What do you know about love? How could you and Tim do this to me? He raped me and beat me up," I said, sobbing. Tears flowed out of my eyes uncontrollably. "I've always tried to protect you and Tim, but you tried to ruin me."

"I'm sorry, Londie, I'm sorry," said CeCe. I felt CeCe putting her arms around me.

"No, no," I said. "Don't touch me."

CeCe put her arms around me again, and held on to me tight.

"Get off me. Get off me!" I said, trying to keep my voice down but thinking that they could hear us. I pushed her off again, but CeCe grabbed on tight again. "CeCe, get off me." But she continued to hold me tight.

"Londie," said CeCe, "you are a good sister. I'm sorry I didn't know that before."

I knew that CeCe was pregnant, and I didn't want to hurt her. My head begin to pound harder. I closed my eyes. How could anybody sleep with the noise we were making? I felt like Daddy must have known all about it. I had had enough. I just lay there with CeCe's arms wrapped around me, and we both cried. I covered my eyes with my pillow until I fell asleep.

The next morning I woke up to the fresh smell of coffee brewing. It was just like I remembered. CeCe was in the bed with me, sound asleep. My eyes felt so tight. I could barely see out of them. I went into the bathroom to wash my face, and then I went into the kitchen to find Daddy reading the newspaper.

"Good morning, sunshine," he said, putting the newspaper down.

"Good morning, Daddy," I said.

"Did you sleep okay?" he said.

"Yes," I said, lying.

"How do you feel this morning?" he said.

"Okay," I said.

"You're going to be all right, Londie," said Daddy. Just then, I felt like I had been right last night. He had heard CeCe and me arguing.

"Yes," I said. I walked over and gave Daddy a hug, and he hugged me back.

"Have some coffee," he said.

"Okay," I said. He took his fingers and wiped the tears from my eyes, even though the tears were still flowing down my face.

He said, "Londie, you did good." What Daddy didn't know was that these tears weren't tears of joy. They were tears of wanting to beat Tim and CeCe up.

I sat down and put sugar and cream in my coffee. We both sipped our coffees. My head was aching so bad. Daddy put his hand on mine and said, "Everything is going to be all right."

I took a deep breath. "I know," I said. "Can I have a pain pill? I have a headache."

Daddy got the pain medicine bottle and gave it to me. I took two pills and continued sipping my coffee. There was still so much pressure on me. My eyes were tight from crying last night, and still the tears kept on falling. Daddy handed me some napkins, and I wiped the tears away. We had talked so much yesterday that, today, I had nothing to say. This morning, we just smiled at each other and sipped our coffees.

There wasn't any hurry this morning. We all had to enroll in school. Sheila walked into the kitchen and kissed me on the head. I got up and gave her a hug, and she hugged me back. Soon the kitchen was full, and we were all set, ready to eat breakfast. I didn't look at my sister and brother. I was so mad at them. I know my lip poked out. Tim asked to bless the food. He said, "Lord, thank you for this food that is prepared for us and the family gathered here. Me, CeCe, and Londie are thankful to be here and have a home. I want to thank my big sister, Londie, for we owe it all to her. If it had not been for her, Lord, we would not be here today. Thank you for Daddy and Sheila and for making it all possible. Amen," he said.

"Amen," everyone echoed.

I couldn't help it, but my jaws were puffy. CeCe and Tim kept looking at me. Daddy and Sheila looked at us with smiles on their faces. Once again, I felt like they had talked, and I was the last to know. I continued to wipe the tears from my eyes. I believed, in my heart, that they were reaching out to me in their own ways, trying to let me know they were sorry. Even though I knew we were siblings, it was going take me a while to get over this hurt. As of that moment, they were still not forgiven.

We all got enrolled in school. Tim got involved in sports. CeCe would be going to maternity school. Sheila took her shopping for maternity clothes. She was a very good stepmom. Daddy soon got custody of us, and I was glad. Sheila finally got CeCe in to see a doctor. She was five months pregnant. The baby was due February 23.

I stopped working at the diaper company because of transportation. I had a little money saved up in the bank anyway, but Daddy said he had my back. I started working on a scholarship to get into college.

What I really loved about living here was that Daddy and Sheila went to church. We all joined church. Tim and I joined the choir, and this was like a dream come true. I believed the Lord had really been watching over us. Without Him, I knew none of this would have been possible. I was so happy. One Sunday, Tim led us all in a song.

Talk With God

I had a talk, with my God one night; I prayed
and hoped for my life to be right
Please God forgive me, I'm ready to take the
stand and receive thee
Oh yes I am, yes I am, my Lord
He said He'll give me a brand new heart; He'll
heal my body and give me a reward

I know I need thee, how else can I be free, I get
down on my knees and pray to my Lord
Oh Lord I know I've truly been blessed, Cause
you chose me from all the rest

I don't know why, but I washed the tears from
my eyes
Oh yes I did, yes I did, my Lord

I want to wear my crown someday, put on my
robe that is not man made
Walk around the streets, that is paved with Gold,
and I'll never, never, never, grow old
I had a talk with my God one night
Choir: Oh yes
Yes I had at talk with my God one night

This song was inspired and written by Mary Ann
Collins in the early years of 2000. She and only
she is the originator.
Sincerely

Mary Ann Collins
06/28/2012

Then there was clapping. I could see Daddy standing up and clapping. Then Sheila stood up. I knew he was proud; so was I. We went out for Sunday dinner to celebrate. I could see the change in Tim and CeCe. I couldn't help it. I guess I had forgiven them. God said, "Forgive."

Soon I would be a senior in high school. I finally had a good friend at school, which made me so happy. Her name was Myra Jones. I actually had fun and enjoyed being a teenager. Everything seemed to be normal now. We had all settled down in our new home. I can't believe it. We are actually a real family now.

As I looked into the mirror, I noticed some gray hairs on my head. Oh, well. I found a pair of scissors and clipped the strands. I had been through so much, but I was glad I had believed that I could get through it. I thought about our mother a lot. I couldn't help but worry about her because she was our mother and she was out there on the streets somewhere. I knew I needed to find her and get her some help. I will talk to Daddy about it, I thought.

Chapter Six

Our Loss

*O*ne evening, Daddy sat watching the news, like he always did after work. Sheila was in the kitchen, cooking, and the rest of us were scattered around and about. The news lady said that a body of a woman had been found in a wooded area. I glanced slowly as I walked by the TV set.

The victim had been identified, but the name was being withheld until the family had been notified. Just then, the phone rang. Daddy answered it. I paused and turned my head to see Tim and CeCe looking too. Daddy dropped the phone and he yelled, "No!" and started crying in his wife's arms. I screamed as I looked around, and everybody was crying, even Sheila. After the shock, Daddy talked to us about the death of our mother; she had been murdered. I thought, of all the people I tried to help, I failed with Momma.

Daddy and Sheila made all the arrangements for the funeral. The following week, we laid Lorna Jeanette Eubank Penn, our momma, to rest. The obituary said she had a sister, who preceded her in death, named Katherine Joyce Eubank.

The last song we sang was "Amazing Grace." Before that, I especially liked the part when we sang, "He Looked Beyond My Fault and Saw My Need." We all could not stop crying. Soon we were on our way to bury Momma.

Even though Momma and I were not close, I still loved her. She would surely be missed.

I finally got to see my momma's parents. Daddy pointed them out to us. It seemed to me that we were strangers to them too. We didn't know them, nor did they know us.

After they stared at us for a while, the services ended. My grandmother came up to me and said, "You always looked like him." I guessed she meant Daddy. CeCe was very much pregnant now, and our grandmother just stared at her and shook her head. My grandfather didn't say a word to us.

Daddy and Sheila stood by us, and we watched them as they walked away. As I suspected, they did not like us. As cold as they were when they came in, they left just the same way.

"Daddy," I asked, "why are they so mean?"

He said, "They never forgave Lorna and me for running off and eloping. They would not give us their blessing. Against their wishes, your aunt, Katherine, asked if she could come and live with us. We said yes because she only wanted to be close to Lorna. She was eighteen years old and had finished high school. Katherine was raped and murdered as she walked home from work one night. They disowned Lorna after that. They said it was all her fault. I tried to help her, but she would not let me. She continued to drink, and we argued all the time. Then one night, we got into this big fight, and she hit me with some brass knuckles. I left that night because I couldn't live that way anymore. So, in order to keep my sanity, I had no choice. That was the saddest day of my life, because I loved her," he said.

"Now I know why she gave up on life and on us, Daddy," I said. "Now I know everything."

Momma may have loved our daddy at one time, but she wept for her sister. Tim pimped his own sister for money. They knew Momma was prostituting.

I never saw the nude pictures of CeCe again. Maybe she trashed them. I turned my head and looked at my brother and sister and thought, I'm glad it's over. We had a chance for a new life, and I was glad. Our mother could not bring her sister back, nor could we bring our mother back, but we were still a family.

One day, at school, as I opened my locker, a fine boy walked up and put his arms around me and said, "Hi, my name is Larry, and I have been watching you. What is your name?"

I turned around and looked at him and said, "My name is Yolonda."

"Do you have a date for the prom?" he said.

"No," I said.

"Would you like to go with me?" he said.

"Larry," I said, "the prom sounds like fun, but I am new at this school, and I don't know why you are asking me."

"Well," he said, "I can't lie; I know you are new. I also know that you are pretty, and I would like to get to know you."

I closed my locker door and turned and looked at him.

"Yolonda," he said, "I'm a good guy. I would like for you to get to know me."

"Larry," I said, "how do you feel about meeting my dad?"

"I will meet him," he said.

Larry came over and met my dad. He liked him and everybody else did too. After the bad experience I had with Arnold, I was glad I was giving Larry Robinson a chance. He was built and fine. He had a car, and I had so much fun with him.

As for CeCe and Tim, who was headed for a job in construction, I believed that having a real home had changed them. They looked happy;

they were staying out of trouble; and they were fun to be around. They also let me in. I was their big sister now. I had so much to be thankful for. We were now officially a family, and that's what I'd always wanted. I chose to hold on to that.

We all got baptized and became members at the Cornerstone Baptist Church. It was like a dream come true for me. I could see Daddy and Sheila, looking so proud.

Two weeks later, on February 20, CeCe had a little boy. She named him Lornell Jerome Penn, in memory of our mother, whom we loved so dearly. He was a handsome little baby whom we all adored even though he was a trick baby, but we wouldn't ever tell. He was our family.

Sheila helped me shop for my prom dress. Larry and I picked the color powder blue. We found a beautiful dress. I tried it on. It was lovely. We found a purse, shoes, and jewelry too. I was all ready for that big day. Larry was ready for the prom as well. The closer we got to the day, the more excited I became.

Finally prom day was here. I got to get my hair fixed in a ball. Sheila helped me get dressed. I looked in the mirror, and for the first time, I felt I was beautiful. It brought a smile to my face. "You look so pretty," said Sheila.

"Thank you, Sheila," I said.

Sheila and Dad made this the happiest day ever for me. It was everything I had dreamed of—everything I had wished for. It all was happening to me. It was like a fairy tale had come true.

I was all ready to go. Larry gave me a corsage. "You look beautiful," he said.

"Thank you; you do too," I said.

"You look so beautiful," said Daddy.

"Thank you, Daddy," and I gave him and Sheila a hug. As I looked around, I could see CeCe waving good-bye to me. She was holding little Jerome.

In the back of my mind, I wished CeCe and I had had this special time to bond. Jerome kept her very busy. I had to admit that CeCe turned out to be a good mom. Of course, she had help from Daddy, Sheila, Tim, and me—the whole family. We were all there for CeCe and Jerome.

Then Sheila started taking pictures of Larry and me as we walked out the door. I could see Tim outside, checking out the limo. Larry took my hand, and we strolled together and got into the limo.

"Have fun," Sheila said.

Tim nodded his head and gave us a thumbs-up. We waved good-bye, and they smiled and waved back. Then finally, the limo drove off. We all waved good-bye.

Larry leaned over and softly kissed me on my cheek. Then I turned to him, and he leaned over and kissed me on my lips. I smiled and thought to myself, I love him.

"I love you," said Larry.

Then my lips began to say, "I love you too." He put his arms around me, and I laid my head on his shoulder.

I was feeling a little nervous as we drove, but being close to Larry's warm body made me feel safe. I knew he would take care of me, and I trusted him.

We didn't say very much to each other; we were both quiet. Spoken words weren't important to me right now. At this moment, I had everything I wanted.

I'm the luckiest girl in the world. I have a wonderful boyfriend who loves me and a family I fought so hard to keep.